Long ago, there were many kinds of dinosaurs.

Stomp!
Clomp!
Tromp!

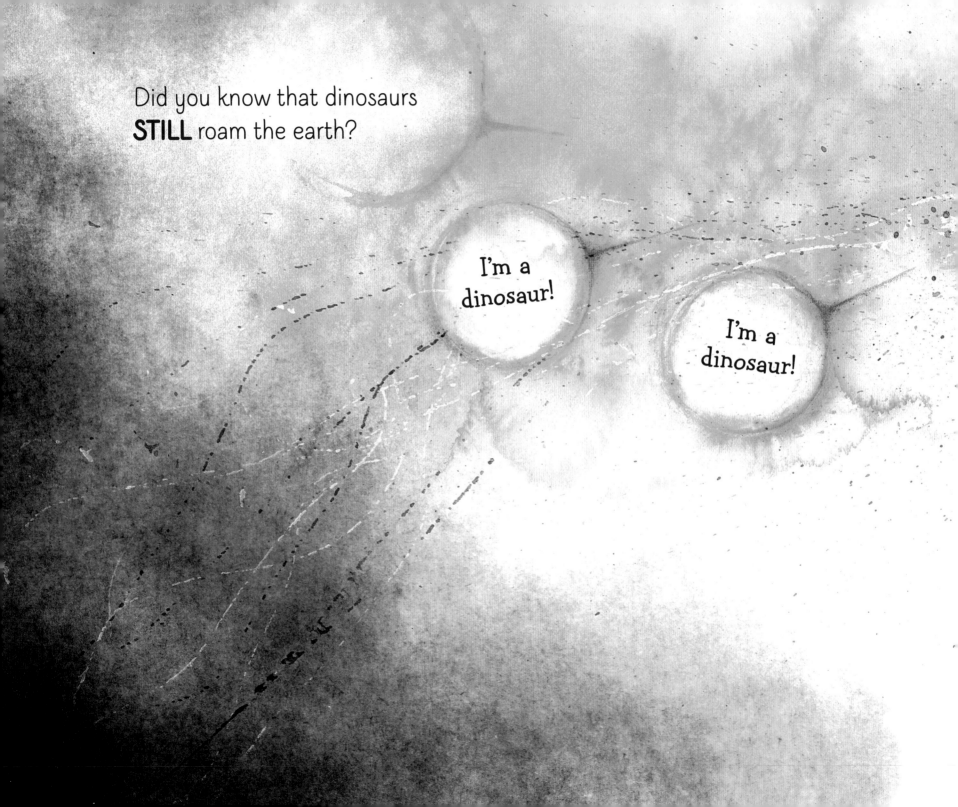

I'm a . . .

Tiny Dino

by Deborah Freedman

VIKING

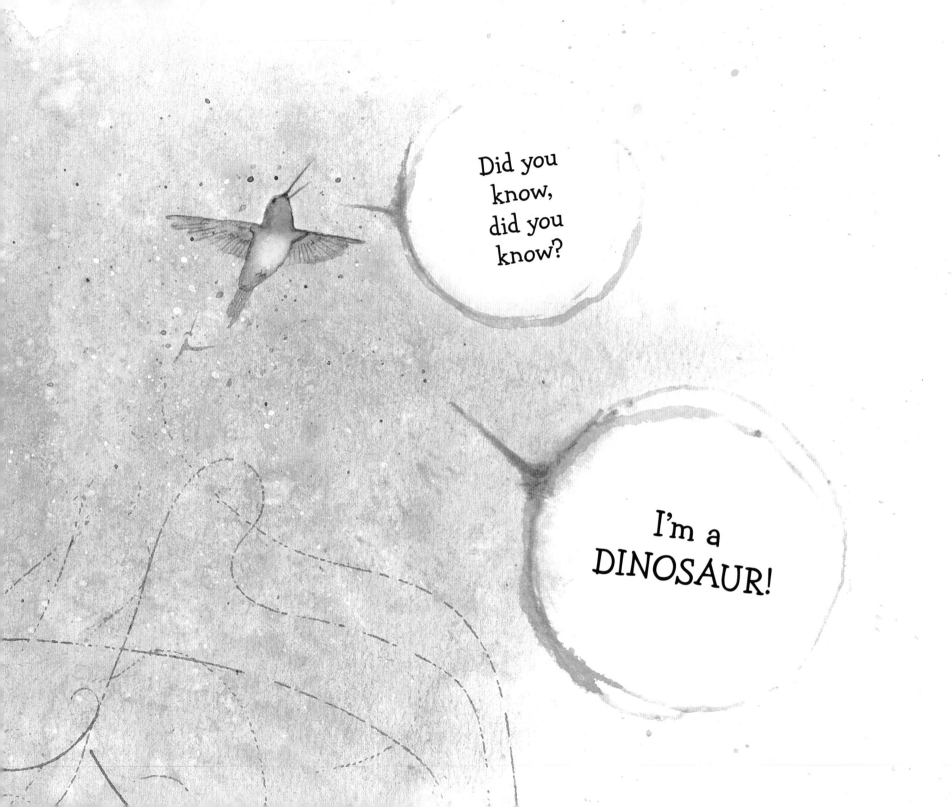

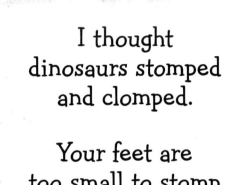

I thought
dinosaurs stomped
and clomped.

Your feet are
too small to stomp
and clomp.

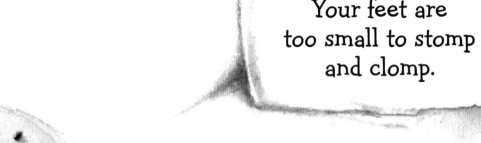

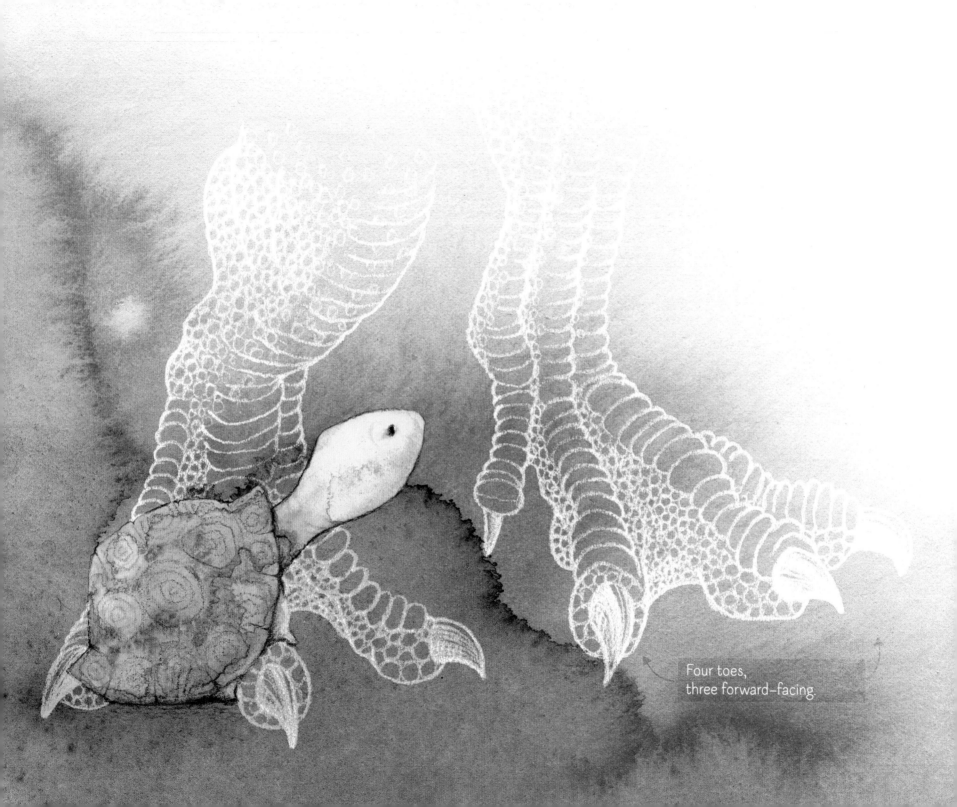

Four toes,
three forward-facing.

Look at my toes!
They are just
like T. rex!

I'm a
dinosaur! I'm
a dinosaur!

But T. rex had
BIG toes.

Yours are little.

And T. rex
had giant
bones.

T. rex had
hollow bones.
And *I* have hollow
bones.

I'm a dinosaur!
I'm a dinosaur!

Some dinosaur and bird bones are
pneumatic—full of hollow spaces
and air. They are light but strong!

Some dinos
had scales and
feathers.

I have
scales and
feathers.

I'm a
DINOSAUR!

FIERCE!

Pardon me!
Did I hear that dinosaurs
still roam the earth?

Aack!
It's a
DINOSAUR!

No. You are not a dinosaur.

But look—
I have scales
on my toes.

And *you*
have scales on
your toes!

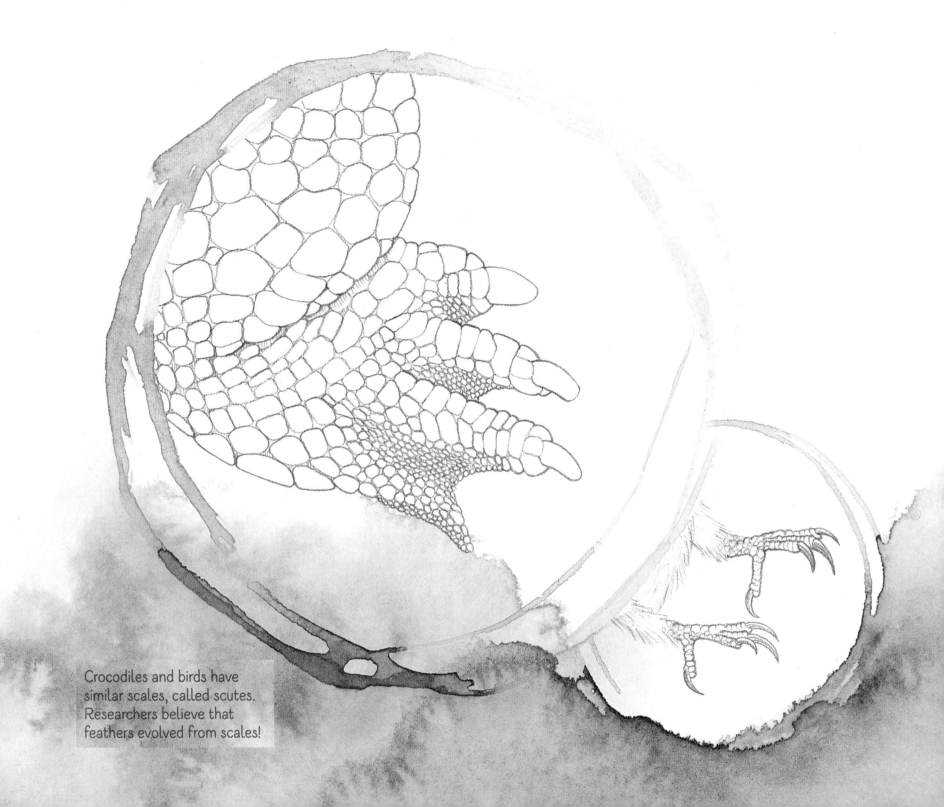

Crocodiles and birds have
similar scales, called scutes.
Researchers believe that
feathers evolved from scales!

I hatched from an egg.
And *you* hatched from an egg!

My heart is like *your* heart!

I sing! You sing!

Four-chambered heart.

Hard-shelled eggs
in a plant-lined nest!

Birds chirp at a high pitch,
and crocodiles hum low.

We are part of the same family tree!

birds!

theropods (extinct)

THEROPODS

ornithischians (extinct)

sauropods (extinct)

DINOSAURS

pterosaurs (extinct)

crocodiles!

snakes

more lizards

lizards

ARCHOSAURS

turtles and tortoises

REPTILES

MAMMALS

Archosaurs were the "ruling reptiles" of the earth about 250 million years ago. They evolved into two main branches: crocodilians and dinosaurs!

AMPHIBIANS

archosaurs (extinct)

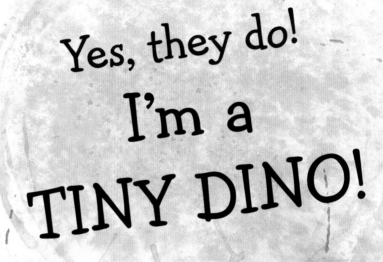

Yes, they do!
I'm a
TINY DINO!

Well.
How about
that.

Author's Note

Did you know that birds really *are* dinosaurs? They share many characteristics. Birds have four toes (three forward-facing), with scales and claws like T. rex! Birds and T. rex both had hollow bones, wishbones, and efficient lungs. Some dinosaurs had feathers. Dinosaurs sat on their eggs to keep them warm and some slept curled up—like birds.

Did you know dinosaurs (including birds), pterosaurs, and crocodilians really *are* related? They are all members of a group of reptiles called archosaurs, and descended from a common agile, running, reptilian ancestor—like a dachshund-sized dinosaur. But 66 million years ago, an enormous asteroid crashed into the earth and most dinosaurs and pterosaurs perished. The world turned dark and resources became scarce. Only a few creatures survived, including some crocodiles, turtles, frogs, small mammals… and avian dinosaurs: birds! Avian dinosaurs evolved into the more than 18,000 species of birds that inhabit our world today.

All living things can be traced back to those that thrived after the last mass extinction, including us. Which species will still be here a million years from now?

Does anybody know?

RESOURCES:
- *Boy, Were We Wrong About Dinosaurs!* by Kathleen V. Kudlinski, illustrated by S. D. Schindler, Dutton Children's Books, 2005
- *Dinosaurs?!* by Lila Prap, NorthSouth Books, 2010
- *Dinosaur Feathers*, by Dennis Nolan, Neal Porter Books/Holiday House, 2019
- *Feathered Dinosaurs*, by Brenda Z. Guiberson, illustrated by William Low, Henry Holt and Company, 2016
- *How Big Were Dinosaurs?* by Lita Judge, Roaring Brook Press, 2013
- *Scaly Spotted Feathered Frilled: How Do We Know What Dinosaurs Really Looked Like?* by Catherine Thimmesh, Houghton Mifflin Harcourt, 2013

For more resources, visit
deborahfreedman.net.

for Sam, our tiniest,
and Otis, Birdie, Roxie, Oliver, & Eliot

Many thanks to Dr. Bhart-Anjan Bhullar of Yale University
and the Peabody Museum of Natural History for generously sharing his expertise.

VIKING
An imprint of Penguin Random House LLC, New York

First published in the United States of America by Viking, an imprint of Penguin Random House LLC, 2022

10 9 8 7 6 5 4 3 2 1

HH

Design by Deborah Freedman and Jim Hoover
Text set in Culinary Sans

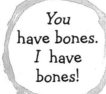

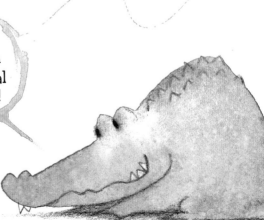